In Someone Else's Shoes

Stephanie Baudet

Illustrated by
Derry Dillon

WITHDRAWN
FROM STOCK

POOLBEG
FOR CHILDREN

Published 2001
by Poolbeg Press Ltd
123 Baldoyle Industrial Estate
Dublin 13, Ireland
E-mail: poolbeg@poolbeg.com
www.poolbeg.com

1 3 5 7 9 10 8 6 4 2

A catalogue record for this book is available from the British Library.

ISBN 1 84223 029 8

Cover design by Steven Hope
Illustrations by Derry Dillon
Set by Patricia Hope in Times 15/21
Printed by The Guernsey Press Ltd,
Vale, Guernsey, Channel Islands.

About the Author

Stephanie Baudet was born in Cheshire, England, and grew up in Australia and New Zealand. After training as a nurse she returned to England and now lives in Buckinghamshire with her husband and two cats. She has a grown up daughter who lives in Australia.

Also by Stephanie Baudet

A Present From Egypt
Double Bubble Trouble

For Jenny

Chapter 1

Nicholas wished it was over. He wished he were anywhere but here. He wished it was three-thirty and he was on his way home. He wished he was tidying his bedroom or washing the dishes. Anything, anything but being here, in school, at this moment.

It was getting closer. It would soon be his turn. He felt his heart begin to thud so much that he was sure other people could see his shirt pounding in and out. Then they would all know he was afraid. He wiped his sweaty hands on his pants and tried to concentrate on the book in front of him, keep his place. His head felt light. Scotty was reading now, then it would be him. He prayed for the bell to go, to be saved by something. Maybe there'd be an earthquake and they'd all have to go outside in an orderly fashion, no panic.

By the time the school had been rebuilt, Mr Cole would have forgotten whose turn it was to read aloud.

But it didn't happen. His chair and table stood rock-solid. Everything stayed normal and Scotty's voice came to a stop with the wave of Mr Cole's hand.

There was an expectant silence as they waited for him, Nicholas Simpson, to begin. He swallowed and his head spun. He heard his voice and it sounded strange, not like part of him at all. His mouth kept filling with spit and he needed to swallow all the time. He tried to finish the sentence first but couldn't do it, the result being a sort of choking.

He heard a snigger from behind and a voice said: "Nickers is getting in a twist again." It was Michael Leewood.

Mr Cole nodded. "Thank you, Nicholas. Next!" And the turbulence settled slowly and his heart resumed its normal tempo. It was over – until the next time.

The bell went and Mr Cole raised his voice above the sudden scraping of chairs and outbreak of chatter.

"BEFORE you go," he said, "homework." There was a groan. "Thoughts about this year's charity concert at the end of term. That gives us just three weeks. Who is going to take part, what you're going to do and above all, which charity we're going to support. Suggestions tomorrow please."

Nicholas never did anything for the charity

concert. He sometimes wondered what it would be like to perform and have an audience applaud. It must be a great feeling to have the spotlight on you and people clapping. Kids played music or recited poems, things like that. He remembered last year Michael Leewood had done a monologue and everyone had fallen about laughing.

"Hey, Nickers!" It was Michael Leewood coming up behind and grabbing his shoulder. "I know what you could do! Cooking! Like

they do on telly." He laughed, coming round in front and blocking his way. Then he said in a posh voice: "And here's one I made earlier."

Nicholas stared at the floor and waited for Michael to move. It was weeks since their Easter fete but they kept on about it. Why had his mother spread it around that he enjoyed cooking and had made the cakes for the stall? What was so wimpish about that? Men were chefs, weren't they? And bakers?

"Come on," said Scotty, tugging his arm, "we'll miss the bus."

"I expect he's going home to cook the dinner," said Michael to two of his mates, who sniggered.

Nicholas examined the cracks in the tarmac of the playground and wished Michael would go away.

He wished he could answer back with some snappy retort, look him in the eye, push him aside and walk away. Most people would do that, but he couldn't. He stood as if he were glued to the spot, heart thumping and fists tightly clenched to stop his hands shaking.

Scotty saved him as usual. He just grabbed his arm and dragged him towards the bus. Michael's laugh followed them right out of the gates and along the road.

The two boys slumped into their seats. Nicholas felt grateful to Scotty for being his friend and sticking with him. He wondered why he *was* his friend.

"What can we do?" asked Scotty, suddenly.

"When?"

"In the concert."

Nicholas shrugged. Scotty knew that he was never in it so why was he asking?

"You should sing," said Scotty, "your mum says you can sing."

"I'm rubbish."

"No, you're not. I heard you once. You sounded brilliant."

"When?"

"That time I came round to borrow your

video of *Space Demons*. You were in your room and you didn't hear me coming."

He remembered. "I'm rubbish," he said again.

To his relief Scotty let it drop. He'd be very careful who heard him singing in future. Scotty had better not tell anyone else about him singing. He opened his mouth to say so but then closed it again. It might give Scotty ideas. Friends couldn't always be trusted.

There was a vote on which charity they should support and the whole school took part during assembly. Nicholas wanted to suggest the RSPCA as he'd seen a film about their work. His heart thudded as he imagined himself putting up his hand and then everyone turning to look. Everyone would probably say scornfully that people were more important than animals.

In the end he voted for the Samaritans. They helped a lot of people who had big problems and needed someone to talk to. The Samaritans won by a large majority. Mrs Peterson, the Head, said she would arrange for someone from that charity to come and talk to them soon so that they would know where the money was going.

"Shame!" said Michael Leewood, passing close to Nicholas as they filed into the classroom. "I bet Nickers wanted it to go to a cooking charity. Are there any cooking charities?" He looked around at his mates with an exaggerated expression of inquiry.

"Save the Sausage Roll?" shrieked David Rowan. Nicholas sat down trying to ignore them and pretending to rummage in his bag for something.

Sunday was boot sale day. Well, not every Sunday but most. Scotty was away at his Gran's this weekend so it was something to do, Nicholas thought, as he pulled on his jacket and followed his mum and dad to the car.

It was at Green Lane Middle School. He sighed as they drove in. Not many stalls. Boring. The usual old junk. He wandered off on his own.

He almost missed them. He would have if he'd turned down the next row of cars instead of going right to the corner. There was no-one at the stall, only the lady running it. That's

what had made him go to look. He couldn't
be bothered fighting through crowds.

On top of a pile of old books they sat, black
and new-looking. The laces were purple-and-
green striped. They were really cool.

"What size are you, son?"

Nicholas almost jumped. Size. That was
important.

"One, I think."

"These are one-and-a-halves. Try them. You can always grow into them."

Nicholas looked at the lady's face then. She was smiling, but sadly, as if she didn't want to part with the shoes.

"They're almost new, only been worn a couple of times." She picked up the Jumping Jacks and held one out to him.

Nicholas dragged off his trainers without undoing the laces and slipped his foot into the shoe. He wiggled his toes around. They were spacious but okay. He put on the other and stared down at them. Real cool!

He looked up but the lady was serving someone else. Suddenly there was quite a crowd round the stall. He didn't have any money. Where were his parents? He looked round anxiously. He'd just have to wait here and hold the shoes until they came. He couldn't risk anyone else buying them.

With a new confidence he called out: "How much are these, please?"

The woman looked up and came to his end of the stall, peering over it at his feet.

"Well, they do fit well. They're five pounds to a good home."

"Can I wait here for my mum?"

"Course you can."

He liked her. She trusted him. She didn't tell him to take them off and she'd look after them until his mum came.

Nevertheless, he did take them off and stood, turning them over and over in his hands. These were really expensive shoes, just what he wanted – and only a fiver!

Chapter 2

Nicholas had the strange feeling, as he walked through the school gates on Monday morning, that he'd grown. How could you grow over one weekend? It was stupid, he knew, yet that was how he felt. He turned to look at Scotty.

"What?" asked his friend.

"Nothing." No, he was still slightly shorter than Scotty. Weird!

Michael Leewood sauntered up. "What's cooking?" He smirked.

Nicholas looked him straight in the eye.

"Oh, a tomato and mushroom pizza, a couple of loaves of bread and . . . a chocolate cake," he said.

Michael was struck dumb. He stood staring with his mouth open like a fish. Nicholas was

surprised himself. It was as if someone else had taken over his body. He looked down at himself. Same thin body, same red jersey, same grey pants, same . . . no, something was different. He held one foot out.

"Like my JJ's?"

All eyes looked at his feet. Scotty noticed them for the first time.

"Cool!" he said. That's what the others were thinking too, Nicholas could tell, but they wouldn't say.

"You won the lottery or something?" asked Michael, finding his voice at last and sounding most unlike his usual self.

Nicholas was about to tell them about the boot sale but then decided not to. They didn't have to know everything. Let them think his parents had paid a lot of money for them. They looked new, anyway.

The bell rang on cue and he walked away, his shoes clomping confidently on the asphalt. Maybe *they* couldn't hear them above the

playground clatter, but he could and it was a good sound.

He continued to surprise himself during the day even though he couldn't understand what had made him change. During the history lesson on the Victorians, he even told the whole class a gruesome story he'd read about how people used to dig up dead bodies, remove the teeth and sell them to dentists to make false teeth. Everyone had made sick noises. Just as well it had been before lunch.

Another thing he did, which he'd probably regret later, was that he'd volunteered to sing for the concert! On his own. All in all, it had been a surprising day.

Nicholas was glad to get home and change into his old trainers. He'd never have admitted it to anyone, but his right ankle felt really sore. There were no blisters or marks anywhere. Maybe he'd twisted it slightly. The funny thing was, when he put his trainers on the pain went. Shrugging, he rubbed a mark off one of the JJs with his finger, breathed on it and polished it with the corner of the duvet.

There was some writing inside which he hadn't noticed before and he peered closer. T O M. It was written in black felt pen round the inside of the heel. TOM. That must be who they'd belonged to before. Why didn't Tom want them any more? For a moment he wondered whether Tom knew something he didn't – like JJs were going out of fashion! Just as he'd got some! But he remembered the reaction at school and dismissed that thought. Nevertheless, he was intrigued to know why Tom should throw them out, and why his mum should let him.

The next day his leg hurt even more. It became so bad that he couldn't help limping; in fact, he could hardly walk at the end of the day. Everyone noticed, of course, and Michael's mate, David Rowan, laughed and said it served him right, but Nicholas had made some retort that had shut him up. Snappy replies seemed to roll off his tongue like peas off a knife, as his dad would say. It was really weird.

"Nicholas! What's the matter? What have you done?" asked his mum as soon as he got home. He'd tried hard to walk naturally through the door but you couldn't hide anything from her.

"Oh, nothing, Mum."

"It's those shoes, isn't it? I knew I shouldn't have bought you someone else's shoes. They can damage your feet."

"It's not the shoes, Mum," he said. "My ankle hurts, not my foot.

"Then I'll take you to the doctor." She looked at her watch. "If we get there early they may squeeze us in."

Nicholas knew he was beaten. He took off the JJs and carried them upstairs. Suddenly his leg was fine!

"It's okay now, Mum. Doesn't hurt at all."

His mum looked up at him from the hall, a doubtful expression on her face.

Just to prove it he ran downstairs and up again in his socks. She seemed convinced then and nodded.

"All right, but you're not to wear those shoes for a couple of days. Give them a rest."

Suddenly the thought of going to school without them filled him with dread. What would the other kids say? What would Michael Leewood say? They'd all laugh at him. Expensive shoes and now he couldn't wear them. He'd never live it down. He'd be more of a target for their jibes than usual.

Nicholas looked at the shoes. Which was worse, the pain they caused if he wore them or the taunting if he didn't? He decided to take them in his schoolbag and put them on when he got there. Maybe his leg would be okay tomorrow.

"Leave those shoes out," said his mum the next morning. "I've had an idea. You know my friend Jean is a chiropodist? I'll take them and ask her advice. If she says they're bad for your feet we throw them out. All right? It's not worth crippling yourself for the sake of fashion."

Nicholas' heart sank. Not only couldn't he take them to school, there was a chance he'd lose them altogether. Nothing ever went right for him!

Chapter 3

"What happened to the shoes, Nickers? Been a naughty boy and your mum's taken them back to the shop?"

Nicholas didn't look at Michael. He stared at the ground a few inches in front of his feet and listened to the other boy's derisive laughter. He felt hollow inside and tears pricked his eyes as he stood, waiting for the ordeal to be over. Waiting until Michael and his hangers-on got tired of baiting him.

But they weren't going to leave until they

got an answer. Michael put out his foot and pushed it against one of Nicholas'.

"Tell us, Nickers. Where are the shoes?" He shoved Nicholas' foot again with his own.

"I've got to get used to them," said Nicholas in a small voice.

There were hoots of laughter again but, much to Nicholas' relief, Michael removed his foot just as the bell rang and they all trudged into the classroom. If only Mum's friend would say the shoes were okay! He couldn't bear it if he could never wear them again. They'd never leave him alone. Still, he sighed, sitting down at his table, if it wasn't the shoes, they'd find something else to bully him about.

At lunch-time there was a rehearsal for the concert to decide who was doing what. Nicholas just couldn't believe he'd agreed to sing. What had made him do it? He tried to pretend he'd never volunteered but there were too many witnesses so he mumbled something about losing his voice.

"It sounds all right to me," said Sam Brown. "Don't just stand there looking stupid."

I'm good at that, thought Nicholas. Standing and looking stupid.

Yesterday he'd really thought he'd changed. He'd enjoyed feeling more confident. But why just yesterday? What had been different about yesterday? The only thing different about yesterday had been the shoes on his feet. How could they possibly make a difference? How could wearing a different pair of shoes make you feel so different inside? It was stupid.

During the afternoon he began to wonder about the shoes. Who was this Tom whose name was inside? It would be interesting to meet him.

What had Mum's friend said about the shoes? Suddenly he couldn't wait to get home and find out. He had to put them on again and see if they really did make a difference to him.

At home time Nicholas didn't wait for Scotty but rushed out to get ahead of Michael Leewood. Luckily the bus was there so he could climb straight aboard. Scotty slumped down beside him.

"You going to wear those shoes tomorrow?" he asked, stretching his feet out along the aisle of the bus and looking at his own battered trainers.

Not the shoes again. Couldn't anyone talk about anything but the shoes?

"Yeah," he answered.

"I told mum about them but she said they're a silly price."

"Yeah."

Scotty sighed and wriggled impatiently on the seat. "Well, how much were they?"

Nicholas knew he would find out in the end. His mum was sure to mention it to Scotty's. "Promise you won't let on."

Scotty nodded, looking at him calmly now, all ears.

"Five pounds."

"What!"

"In a boot sale."

His friend grinned widely. "Oh, right," he said.

Nicholas almost told him about the name inside. Tom. And how the shoes seemed to change him. But it would sound silly. He'd keep it to himself for the moment. Some things were better kept to yourself.

When he pushed open the back door the shoes were the first things he saw. They were on the worktop in the kitchen, neatly standing side by side, shiny bits shining, suede bits rich and warm, coloured laces cheerfully strewn in haphazard fashion. They really were seriously good, those shoes, he thought. Really, really . . .

"It's all right, Nicholas. You can wear them." His mum was smiling when he turned to look at her. She was great, his mum. He wanted to hug her but didn't move.

"Jean says they're fine. They are a good shape and they have hardly been worn by the previous owner so they haven't moulded to their foot shape. In fact, she can't understand why they hurt."

"Oh, it's nothing, Mum." He'd wear them if they were agony, even if his foot dropped off. Nothing was going to stop him now.

"Take your old shoes to school as well," his mum was saying, "then you can change if they hurt."

Nicholas knew it was easier to nod and not argue. But those shoes were staying on his feet ALL DAY.

He was ten feet tall again the next day. At least, that's how it felt. School was even enjoyable now. He wasn't any cleverer but he was eager to join in more and that made it more interesting. He asked questions, he gave answers, he even sang in the rehearsal. It was amazing!

And he decided to find the owner of the shoes.

It had been a sudden decision, more like a compulsion. He had to find out what this Tom was like and why he didn't want the shoes. It shouldn't be difficult, he knew which school he probably went to. The only problem was getting over there as they were coming out, and that meant leaving here early and he wasn't quite sure how he was going to do that. His mum would be mad when he was late home. He'd have to run all the way, all two miles of it. Nicholas wasn't even sure he could run two miles.

"Got used to your shoes?" asked Michael Leewood, giving Nicholas' foot a nudge with his own as he passed to go to his table. It was almost a kick but not quite. "Not hurting you any more, then?"

"No," lied Nicholas, smiling sweetly at him. "They're fine. Very comfortable." He wished he'd put out his foot first and tripped him up. No-one was going to kick these shoes!

Michael looked a bit puzzled for a moment but then walked off with an exaggerated swagger. Nicholas watched him and thought how his view of Michael had changed so much. He couldn't imagine how he had ever been afraid of him. He could even admit that now. He *had* been afraid of him. Only yesterday he'd stood like a wally while Michael baited him. Yesterday, when he hadn't been wearing the shoes.

Shoes or not, there was no reason to be afraid of Michael or anyone else.

"I'm not catching the bus home," he said to Scotty just before the home-time bell went.

"How are you getting home?"

He was tempted again to tell Scotty about trying to find Tom. Maybe he would come to the school with him. It would be easier with two. But he knew Scotty wouldn't come. And maybe he'd think it was a stupid idea. Maybe it *was* a stupid idea. He'd tell him later after he'd met Tom. Then there'd be something to tell.

"I've got to go somewhere first, then I'll walk."

Scotty looked at him, waiting for an explanation and when it didn't come he just shrugged and turned back to the history project they were supposed to be doing. Nicholas could see that he was in danger of losing a friend if he was so secretive. He'd definitely tell him tomorrow.

It was difficult trying to concentrate on the Voyages of Sir Francis Drake when he was looking at his watch every minute. It was like being in a race and crouching on the starting blocks, waiting for the starting pistol. At a quarter past three he started putting his pen and pencils away, then his book. As soon as the bell went he'd be first out of the classroom, grab his coat and away. Never mind putting the chairs up. Never mind anything else. He'd have maybe ten minutes to run the three-quarters of a mile to Green Lane Middle School.

His muscles were tense. The hands of the wall-clock staggered round to twenty past. Then the bell went and he was off, charging like a bull, through the door and into the corridor as if a wild animal were after him.

He must be mad, he thought, as he raced through the school gates. What was this all for? The shoes still hurt too, at least the right one did, just as much as ever. He wished now that he'd taken his mum's advice and brought his old trainers.

Chapter 4

It was the same familiar scene outside Green Lane School. Children milling around, mums standing chatting at the gates, rows of cars, noisy crowds pushing onto buses and slinging their bags onto the overhead racks.

Nicholas stood getting his breath back and rubbing his right ankle. The pain was almost unbearable. He loosened the laces and slipped his foot out for a moment. Immediately there was relief. He waggled his toes and then put his foot half in the shoe. Everyone would be gone if he didn't hurry.

Where to start? Who should he ask? Looking round he targeted someone who looked about his own age.

"Hey, do you know someone called Tom?"

The girl looked back at him over her shoulder.

"Tom who?"

"I dunno."

She shrugged and walked off.

There was no sign of the woman from the stall where he'd bought the shoes either. Maybe Tom walked home or went on the bus.

He asked one or two other people and got no satisfactory answer. He even asked a couple of mums who broke off their chatting to smile at him and shake their heads. They didn't really look at him or listen. Nobody was interested.

The crowd was getting thinner. Cars were starting up and driving away, buses leaving. He thought of his own bus on its way home without him on it. He thought of his mum looking at her watch when he didn't arrive at the usual time. Worrying. Phoning Scotty. This whole thing had been a waste of time and he'd be in trouble too.

Well, it wouldn't be a waste of time. He walked decidedly through the school gates and up to the main entrance.

He'd have to ask a teacher.

"Tom?" said the teacher he met in the corridor. "I don't think we have anyone called Tom. Why do you want him?"

Nicholas explained about the shoes. Not everything of course, just about wanting to meet the owner and thank him. Something like that. The teacher seemed to accept his reason and stared vacantly ahead as he thought.

He shook his head. "No, definitely no Tom. It was at our boot sale, you say? Where was the stall? I might remember who it was as I was one of the organisers."

"It was at the end, in the corner by the gate. A lady with glasses and short dark hair."

Recognition dawned on the teacher's face. "Mrs O'Malley it must have been. But there's no-one called Tom that I know of, it's Terry."

"Could you tell me where they live, please?"

The teacher opened his mouth to speak but then closed it again and looked closely at Nicholas through his thick glasses as if seeing him for the first time.

"I'm not sure I can do that, son. I don't know you, do I? And I don't know any Tom." He shook his head, his mind made up. "Sorry son. Bring a note from your mum and I might consider it, but otherwise, I can't go giving out people's addresses to strangers."

Nicholas had to accept that. At least he had a name. Terry O'Malley. He pushed through the doors and began to run.

He told the truth to his mum. It was the only thing to do. He got the inevitable lecture but she wasn't as cross as he'd thought she would be.

"How are the shoes today?"

"Fine, thanks."

She smiled. "Good. You'd have been disappointed if you couldn't wear them, wouldn't you?"

Disappointed was an understatement.

He grabbed the telephone book and took it up to his room and flung it onto the bed. What a relief to get the shoes off! He'd never had shoes hurt him so much before.

O'Malley. Nicholas opened the book and began looking through the Os.

There were five O'Malleys. One of the addresses he knew was a long way from Green Lane School. His dad had a friend who lived in that road.

That left four. He would have to ring them all up and just ask for Terry. The thought of telephoning strangers made his heart thump. He stared at the print on the page until it went all blurry. Maybe he should forget this whole thing. If he found Terry what was he going to say to him?

"I've got your shoes. I wondered why you got rid of them."

He hung his head over the edge of the bed and stared at the shoes on the floor. Then he

got up quickly and slipped his feet into them, picking up the phone book and scuffling to the door without doing up the laces.

If he didn't do it, it would keep nagging at him, he knew. So, what was wrong with talking to strangers on the phone? They didn't know him, did they?

He picked up the receiver and pushed the buttons.

"Could I speak to Terry, please?"

"Terry?"

"Oh, I must have the wrong number. Sorry."

One done, three to go.

The third person to reply was a woman. She didn't answer immediately when he asked for Terry. Then she said:

"Who are you?"

Nicholas explained about the shoes and she laughed. "Oh yes, they were Terry's. How are you getting on with them?"

"They're great."

"Terry will be pleased." She paused again. "Terry is in hospital with a seriously injured leg. That's why I sold the shoes. They'll be too small by now."

Nicholas didn't know what to say.

"It was a road accident two months ago," went on Mrs O'Malley. "It's meant a lot of pain and operations . . ." She stopped again.

"Tell Terry the shoes have a good home," said Nicholas, remembering her words at the boot sale.

Surprisingly, she laughed again. "I will. Or better still, why don't you do it yourself? I'm going to the hospital tomorrow if you'd like to come with me. Terry could do with some cheering up."

They arranged to meet the following afternoon at half past three. Mrs O'Malley spoke to his mum and promised to bring him home afterwards.

Poor Terry! In hospital for two months. He didn't think anyone ever stayed in hospital that long. All that time off school too!

There were a lot of questions to ask Terry, and one in particular.

Chapter 5

"I had to look out for the shoes," laughed Mrs O'Malley. "I'd forgotten what you looked like."

Nicholas smiled. He had remembered her but he didn't say. He'd recognised her straight away, standing near the other mums. She was taller than most of them.

They walked along the path and stopped at a green Peugeot and he waited while she went round to unlock the passenger door.

"Terry doesn't know you're coming," she said, clipping her seat belt. "It'll be a surprise."

I hope he won't be cross, thought Nicholas, not sure how he would feel if his mum brought a stranger to see him and he wanted his mum to himself. If it didn't go well he couldn't leave either, as Mrs O'Malley was taking him home.

They walked though the large entrance hall and made straight for the lifts.

"Have you been in a hospital before?" asked Mrs O'Malley, pushing the up button.

He shook his head.

"This is a very good one," she said as they got in the lift and headed for the third floor.

Nicholas hadn't known there were good ones or bad ones. In fact, he'd never thought much about it at all. It did seem like a friendly place. A nurse greeted Mrs O'Malley with a smile and spoke to her for a minute. Then she was pushing open a door and Nicholas was following her and had a glimpse of a bed with a white cover and the two wheels at the foot were raised onto high wooden blocks.

Mrs O'Malley scooped the person in the bed into her arms. "I have a surprise visitor for you, Terry, dear. The person who bought your shoes. This is Nicholas."

She unwrapped her arms and stood back so that Nicholas could see Terry for the first time. He opened his mouth to say hello but nothing came out. Terry sat grinning widely at him, her long reddish hair spread over the pillows in a tangle.

"Don't worry, my leg's covered up. You won't see anything gory," she said.

"No, it's not that." He found his voice at last. "I thought you were a boy."

Terry and her mum looked at each other and burst out laughing.

"Didn't I say?" asked Mrs O'Malley.

"Terry," said Terry. "It's short for Teresa."

"Oh."

"Are you disappointed? I bet you are. You wouldn't have come if you'd known I was a girl, would you?"

He didn't know. It had just not occurred to him. "Yes, I would." he said.

Terry laughed. She had a high giggle that made him want to smile too. "Liar," she said.

Then her eyes dropped to his feet and her smile faded.

"I'm glad you've got my JJs," she said in a quiet voice. He thought she sounded sad and sorry that she'd had to give them away.

"By the time I can walk again they'd have been too small. Still," she brightened, "Mum's going to buy me another pair, aren't you, Mum?"

Her mum smiled and nodded.

There was the other question he wanted to ask, just to get everything straight.

"Why did you write the name Tom in your shoes?"

She laughed again. "It's my initials. Teresa O'Malley. TOM"

The mystery was over. There was no Tom. Just Terry. A girl called Terry. Nicholas sat down in a chair by the bedside and they began to find out more about each other.

When they left he promised to visit often. Her mum offered to bring him any time he wanted. Sometime he would tell her about how different he felt when he was wearing the shoes, and how miserable he'd been at school before. He'd tell her about singing in the concert and about how he enjoyed cooking.

Something niggled at his brain as they walked back towards the car and it wasn't until he was walking into his own front door that he realised what it was.

The shoes didn't hurt any more.

Chapter 6

Scotty had raised his eyebrows when Nicholas told him about the effect the shoes had on him. It was the sort of quizzical look which questioned whether his friend was right in the head.

"You're bonkers," he said. "How can shoes make you a different person?"

They were on the bus on the way to school. Nicholas shrugged. "I dunno but they do. I have changed, haven't I? I'm different?"

Scotty had to agree.

"They were Terry's shoes. She liked them so much she must have left a part of herself inside them which makes me like her when I wear them. I even had a pain in my right ankle like her."

"Not as bad as hers," said Scotty.

"Course not. Her leg was really smashed up into lots of pieces. They had to pin them all together with bits of wire."

Scotty screwed up his face.

"She's got to start trying to walk soon and she's really scared. She thinks she might not ever be able to walk properly again."

Nicholas was sure she would, and he told her so on his next visit.

She seemed like a different person from the bubbly one he'd met a week ago. Her eyes were dull and her mouth just a thin line. She

was slumped in the bed and didn't answer him, just turned her head as if it were a great effort and looked at him with bleak eyes.

Mrs O'Malley fussed about with the get-well cards and picked the dead flowers out of a vase.

Nicholas began to wish he'd never come. It was silly sitting here with nothing to say.

Her mum settled down at last and sat in the other chair, reaching out to hold Terry's hand.

"Be brave, love. Everything's going to be all right." She glanced up at Nicholas then. "They're going to get Terry up tomorrow and try her on crutches."

Terry still said nothing but sunk further down into the bed.

"I always wanted to have a go on crutches," said Nicholas. "My uncle hurt his ankle and had to have crutches and he could go really fast. The worst thing was going up and down stairs. He said it was really scary, especially going downstairs, and in the end it was easier to shuffle down on his bum."

A small smile broke out on Terry's face like the sun coming from behind a cloud.

"Can I have a go on your crutches?" he asked.

She nodded. "Can you come tomorrow?"

He glanced at her mum.

"Of course," said Mrs O'Malley. "We'll look forward to seeing how you've got on. The doctor says as soon as you can get around on the crutches you can come home."

Terry cheered up a bit after that and they talked about school and his charity concert and about the JJs. When her mum had gone out to have a cup of tea he even told her about how they made him more confident when he wore them, more like her, so that he wasn't afraid to speak up in class or answer back to Michael Leewood.

She even laughed then. "You don't want to be like me," she said. "I get so miserable sometimes and I give up easily. Mum says

I've no patience. I bet you're not like that. And you're good at cheering people up."

They smiled at each other and Mrs O'Malley came back into the room and picked up her coat.

"That's better," she said, looking at Terry. "You're good for her, Nicholas. See you tomorrow, love, and good luck."

The rehearsals for the concert were going well and Nicholas was enjoying himself. He'd meant to think of Terry the next day, taking her first steps on the crutches. He'd meant to try and send her encouraging thoughts. But it wasn't until half past two when they were going into the hall for PE that he remembered and he felt bad about it. It would probably be all over now, but just in case it wasn't, he concentrated hard.

"Nicholas! Wake up! It's your turn!"

He blinked and realised it was Mr Cole speaking. You couldn't have a minute to yourself.

As he ran to do a forward roll on the mat he heard the familiar laugh from Michael Leewood but he didn't let it put him off. It was only after he was on his way back to the line, ignoring Michael, unconcerned, that he realised that, of course, he wasn't wearing the JJs. He had his trainers on.

Michael reached out as he passed and gave him a slight shove and Nicholas cowered away defensively and joined the end of the line.

Five minutes before the bell there was a scramble for the changing rooms and as Nicholas approached his heap of clothes on the bench he knew that something was wrong. There was a space on the floor that shouldn't have been there. A space that should have been filled with his JJs.

Someone had nicked them!

He looked round hastily. No-one was taking any notice of him. All were thrusting arms into shirts and coats and pushing out of the doors. One person in particular was not there at all.

"What's the matter?" asked Scotty.

"My JJs," said Nicholas.

Scotty looked down at his feet. "Where are they?"

GONE!

"They've been nicked!"

Scotty looked sympathetic for a moment. "Tell Mr Cole tomorrow. We can't hang around now or we'll miss the bus."

"I'm not catching the bus. I'm going to see Terry."

He was in Mrs O'Malley's car just pulling out into the road when something caught the corner of his eye.

It was Michael Leewood, grinning widely and holding something up for him to see.

The missing JJs.

Chapter 7

Terry noticed straight away that he wasn't wearing the JJs. She was sitting in a chair today, at the side of her bed.

"Are they hurting you again?" she asked.

He was tempted to lie. How could he admit to them being stolen? Well, he knew who had them and he'd challenge Michael Leewood tomorrow.

Terry's eyes were fixed on him and he knew he had to tell the truth. She'd know if he were lying. He wished she hadn't noticed. He wanted to know how she'd got on with the crutches.

"Michael Leewood took them while we were doing PE"

She looked cross. "You get them back! I don't want *him* to have them."

He felt that she was cross with him and he stood, staring at the floor, all the old feelings coming back.

"Nicholas!"

He looked up.

"Get them back." Her voice was gentler. "You're not afraid of him any more."

He wanted to tell her that he *was* afraid, because he wasn't wearing the shoes any more. How could he stand up to Michael without the shoes? But he just shrugged.

He was aware of Mrs O'Malley sitting quietly and patiently but now she leaned forward and kissed her daughter on the cheek.

"Leave Nicholas alone," she said. She pulled the other chair round. "Come and sit down, Nicholas. We want to hear how the walking got on, don't we?"

Terry's face closed a little. "Okay," she said.

"What do you mean, okay?" said her mum, "What did it feel like? How far did you go?"

"It was my first time up, Mum. I went about five steps and my good leg felt like jelly. The crutches slip on the floor too." She looked at Nicholas. "I don't believe your uncle went very fast. You were just saying that!"

"I wasn't! You've just got to get used to them."

"I'll *never* get used to them," she said. "I'll be in here for *ever*."

Nicholas looked round, still eager to have a go. "Where are they?"

"The physios took them away again."

"Physios?"

"They help you to walk and teach you exercises and things." She looked at him, her shoulders hunched up. "I'm sure you could walk with them very well, Nicholas. It's easy when you have two good legs if you lose your balance but I'm not allowed to put any weight on this leg at all for another four weeks."

He grinned. "So after four weeks you can start really walking again?"

She nodded.

"So after today it'll only be twenty-seven days. You can do a count-down. It'll soon go!"

"I'll cross the days off a calendar for you," said her mum.

Terry brightened. "Right," she said. "You've cheered me up again, Nicholas."

He felt pleased as they went home. At least he was good at something.

Two things happened as they arrived at school the next day and they both had to do with Michael Leewood.

The first thing was that he was wearing the JJs but he had put in some different laces.

The second was that he knew about Terry.

"Been to visit your girlfriend yesterday?" he asked, sauntering to meet them as they stepped off the bus.

How did he know about Terry? The only person who knew about her was Scotty. Nicholas turned to his friend. Scotty blushed and shrugged.

"Didn't know it was a secret," he muttered.

So Michael Leewood had got to Scotty too. He must have seen him getting into Mrs O'Malley's car and asked Scotty about it. Scotty, who he thought was not afraid of Michael!

He turned back to Michael. "So what?" he said. "And you're wearing *my* shoes."

Michael put on an expression of mock surprise. "Your shoes? These are mine. Mum bought them for me yesterday. Don't blame me if you lost your shoes."

"I can prove they're mine," said Nicholas. "They've got some initials inside."

"There's nothing inside these except my name," said Michael, pulling one shoe off without undoing the laces. "See."

He held out the shoe and Nicholas peered

inside. Where the letters T O M had been, there was now a name-badge bearing the letters M A L.

"See," said Michael again. "Mum got them second-hand, hardly used. I don't lie and say they're new."

Nicholas felt beaten. It was no use going to Mr Cole. Michael would just stick to his story and he, Nicholas, couldn't prove a thing. What was Mum going to say, too? She hadn't noticed last night and he hadn't had the courage to tell her.

Suddenly he felt very alone. Even his friend Scotty had betrayed him. He had been bullied into telling about Terry. He wasn't so tough after all, he just pretended to be.

Nicholas realised then that he himself had just stood up to Michael without even thinking about it – and without the shoes. He had been so mad that he'd forgotten his fears. Speaking of which, Saturday night was the concert and unless he got the JJs back in time, he would have to get up on the stage and perform without them. The thought struck fear into him like a knife.

Chapter 8

The hall was filling quickly, row after row of people filed in, taking off jackets and draping them over the backs of the chairs, sitting down and talking to neighbours or reading the programmes which had been handed to them at the entrance.

Nicholas watched through a crack in the curtain with heart thumping. He could have pretended to be ill or something. He still could.

"We regret to announce that Nicholas Simpson is not well . . ."

The audience would feel sorry for him.

"Nicholas!" It was Mr Cole. "Come away. We're about to open the curtains."

If he was going to say something he had to do it now.

He backed away into the wings to wait his turn. He wasn't going to be a coward this time.

When it was time he walked out onto the stage, knees shaking, mouth dry. The lights shone into his eyes. He stood in front of the microphone and began.

In no time it was all over. He'd done it! On his own without the shoes! He felt like a different person as he stood grinning while the audience applauded.

When the concert was over everyone went into a smaller room for tea and biscuits. As he went through the door looking for his mum and dad someone was crossing the floor towards him. Slowly but confidently, swinging her injured leg between the two crutches.

"Terry!"

She laughed. "Surprise! They let me go home yesterday and I've been practising all day today!"

Nicholas didn't know what to say. He just looked at Terry's happy face.

"Thanks," she said.

"What for?"

"For helping." Her smile vanished suddenly and she looked past him, then whispered in his ear. He swung round to see Michael Leewood coming in.

Michael looked at her and then Nicholas, grinning.

"I'll have my shoes back now, please," said Nicholas.

Michael sighed. "We've been through all this before, Nickers. These are my shoes."

Nicholas moved a little closer to him. "I can prove it," he said. "Take one off before I call Mr Cole."

Michael shrugged and did so and Nicholas peeled back the insole at the heel end.

"This is you, is it?" He handed the shoe back and watched Michael's face change.

Under the insole, as Terry had whispered to him, a label was firmly stuck to the bottom of the shoe. It read:

Teresa O'Malley,
26 Fern Crescent,
Bickerton.

"Mum insisted on a hidden name," said Terry. "They were expensive shoes and she thought this might happen."

Without saying another word, Michael took off the other shoe and handed it to him.

"You were good," said Terry, as they watched Michael walk away in his socks.

"But I . . ."

"In the concert, I mean. And without the shoes. That just proves you imagined the effect they had on you."

"Maybe," said Nicholas, and they went to join their parents and get a drink of coke.

THE END